A day with the
Animal Doctors

Sharon Rentta

ALISON
GREEN

Today Terence is feeling
Especially Important.
He is going to be a doctor.

His mummy's going to be a doctor, too, like she always is.

Dr Terence packs his
First Aid Kit . . .

. . . then he shows Mummy
the way to the hospital.
Hospitals are Very Busy.

There are lots of patients in the waiting room.
Waiting can be quite Boring . . .

. . . so Dr Terence shows them
his best dance moves.

Everyone feels much better after that,

except for the cleaning mice.

Some patients
need to see a doctor.

There's Dr Yak,

Dr Zebra,

Dr Chimp,

Dr Mummy

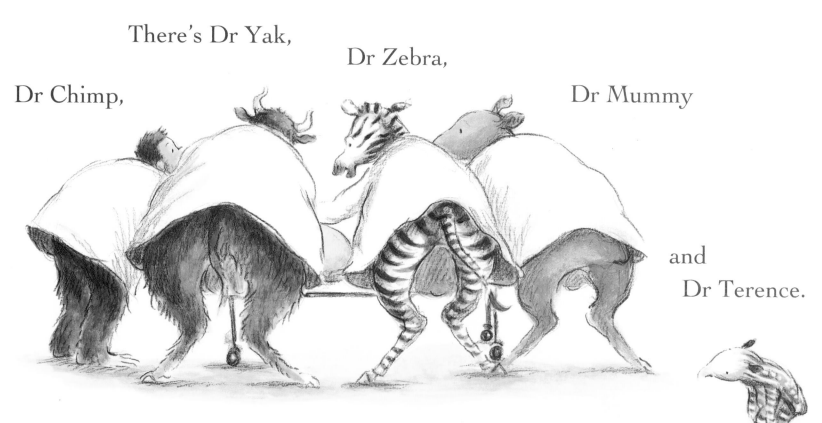

and
Dr Terence.

All the doctors have tails except Dr Chimp.

These are some of the
things that doctors use
to make people better:

a stethoscope,

a bandage,

a watch,

a syringe,

a thermometer

and a nice
cup of tea.

They also use Bedside Manner,
which means being nice to people.
Dr Terence has an Especially
Good Bedside Manner.

They can make the Biggest Fuss.

Some patients are only little.
They often need to do a lot of Bouncing.

It's important for doctors to
do Bouncing, too.

But sometimes
even doctors can
have accidents.

Then they need three things:

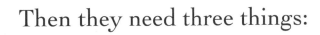

a Cuddle,

a Sticking Plaster

and a Lollipop.

At the end of a long day,
doctors get tired. Then
they have to go home . . .

for a bath,

and a bedtime story.

But a good doctor is
never really off duty.

It's hard work being a doctor.

Night-night, Dr Terence.

For the Hori family,
and for Dr Li Tee,
and Nurse Ginny

First published in 2011 by Alison Green Books
An imprint of Scholastic Children's Books
Euston House, 24 Eversholt Street
London NW1 1DB
A division of Scholastic Ltd
www.scholastic.co.uk
London ~ New York ~Toronto ~ Sydney
Auckland ~ Mexico City ~ New Delhi ~ Hong Kong

Copyright © 2011 Sharon Rentta

HB ISBN: 978 1 407116 46 4
PB ISBN: 978 1 407116 44 0
All rights reserved
Printed in Singapore

9 8 7 6 5 4 3 2 1

Moral rights asserted.

Papers used by Scholastic Children's Books
are made from wood grown in sustainable forests.